3 4028 08796 5043
HARRIS COUNTY PUBLIC LIBRARY

JPIC Oconne
O'Connell, Rebecca
Baby party
WITHDRAWN
$15.99
ocn891001482
08/12/2015

W9-AOS-783

Baby Party

Rebecca O'Connell   Illustrated by Susie Poole

Albert Whitman & Company
Chicago, Illinois

Clap for the babies!
It's a baby party.

Clap for the baby

wearing a triangle.

Clap for the baby

giving a square.

Clap for the baby

playing with a rectangle.

Clap for the baby

sharing
a star.

Clap for the baby

holding an oval.

Clap for the babies

sitting in a circle.

Singing!
Smiling!

At the **baby party**.

To Sally—RO
To Jess, the "jam in the middle!"—SP

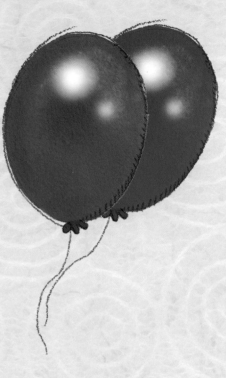

Library of Congress Cataloging-in-Publication Data

O'Connell, Rebecca.
Baby party / Rebecca O'Connell ; illustrated by Susie Poole.
pages cm
Summary: "A baby party introduces toddlers to basic shapes"—Provided by publisher.
[1. Shape—Fiction. 2. Babies—Fiction. 3. Parties—Fiction.] I. Poole, Susie, illustrator. II. Title.
PZ7.O2167Bb 2015
[E]—dc23
2014034301

Text copyright © 2015 by Rebecca O'Connell
Illustrations copyright © 2015 by Albert Whitman & Company
Published in 2015 by Albert Whitman & Company
ISBN 978-0-8075-0512-0

All rights reserved. No part of this book may be reproduced or transmitted in any
form or by any means, electronic or mechanical, including photocopying,
recording, or by any information storage and retrieval system, without
permission in writing from the publisher.

Printed in China
10 9 8 7 6 5 4 3 2 NP 20 19 18 17 16 15
Design by Ellen Kokontis

For more information about Albert Whitman & Company,
visit our web site at www.albertwhitman.com.

Harris County Public Library
Houston, Texas